Dear Daddy...

For Sylvie
in memory of life at Earls Down Farm

This paperback edition first published in 2002 by Andersen Press Ltd.

First published in Great Britain in 1985 by Andersen Press Ltd., 20 Vauxhall Bridge Road, London SW1V 2SA.
Published in Australia by Random House Australia Pty., 20 Alfred Street, Milsons Point, Sydney, NSW 2061.
 Colour separated in Switzerland by Photolitho AG, Zurich.
Printed and bound in Italy by Grafiche AZ, Verona.

10 9 8 7 6 5 4 3 2

British Library Cataloguing in Publication Data available.

ISBN 1 84270 165 7

This book has been printed on acid-free paper

Dear Daddy...

PHILIPPE DUPASQUIER

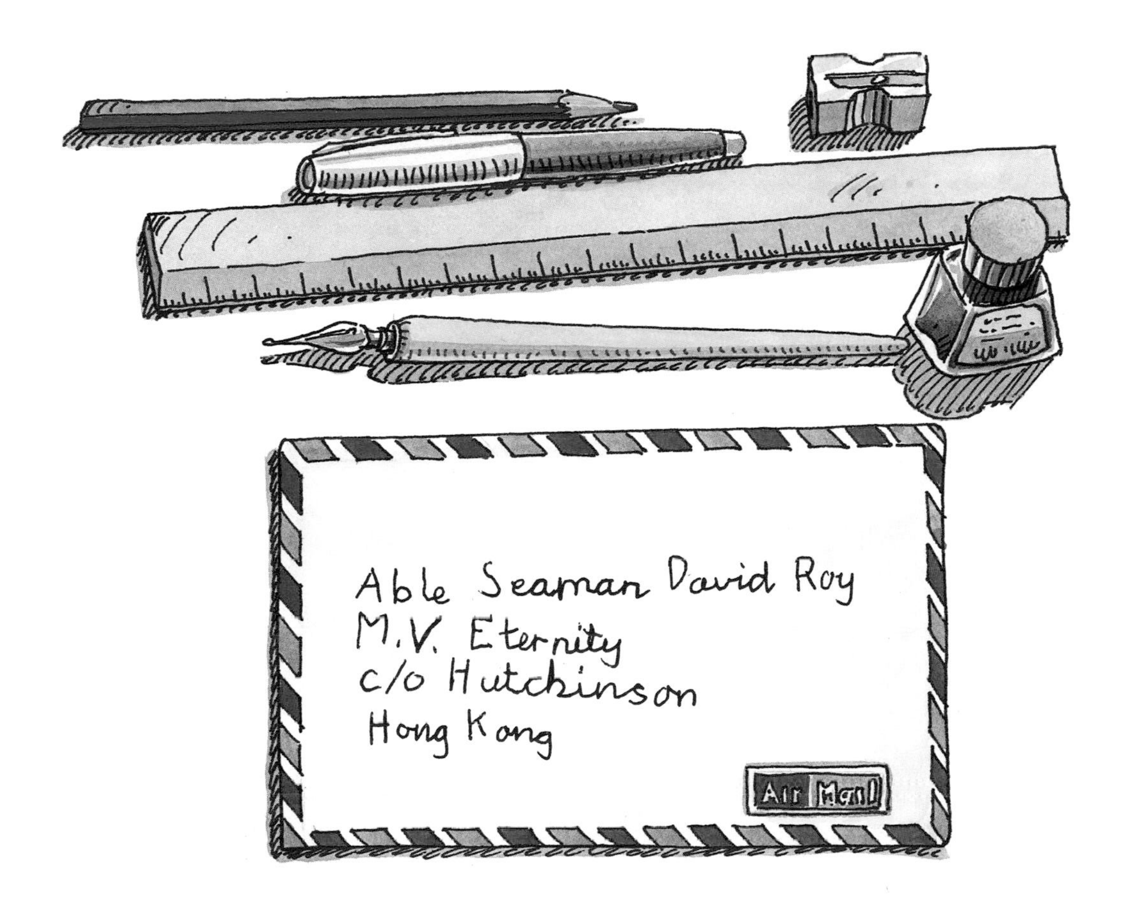

Andersen Press · London

Dear Daddy,
I think about you lots and lots. Are you all right on your ship? We all miss you.

It’s raining all the time at home, so Mummy bought me
some red gumboots. They’re brill!

Mr Green the gardener came to trim the hedge today.
Timmy's got a new tooth. He's got six altogether now.

Mummy says he'll soon be walking. I hope you are well. We think about you all the time.

I had a great birthday party. All my friends came, except for Jacky 'cos she had chicken-pox. Mummy made a chocolate cake.

I had lots and lots of presents. My best one was a mask
for looking underwater when we go to the sea.

School has started again. The garden is full of dead leaves. The teacher showed me on a big map where you are going on your ship.

She said it was a very long way. I wish you were home again.

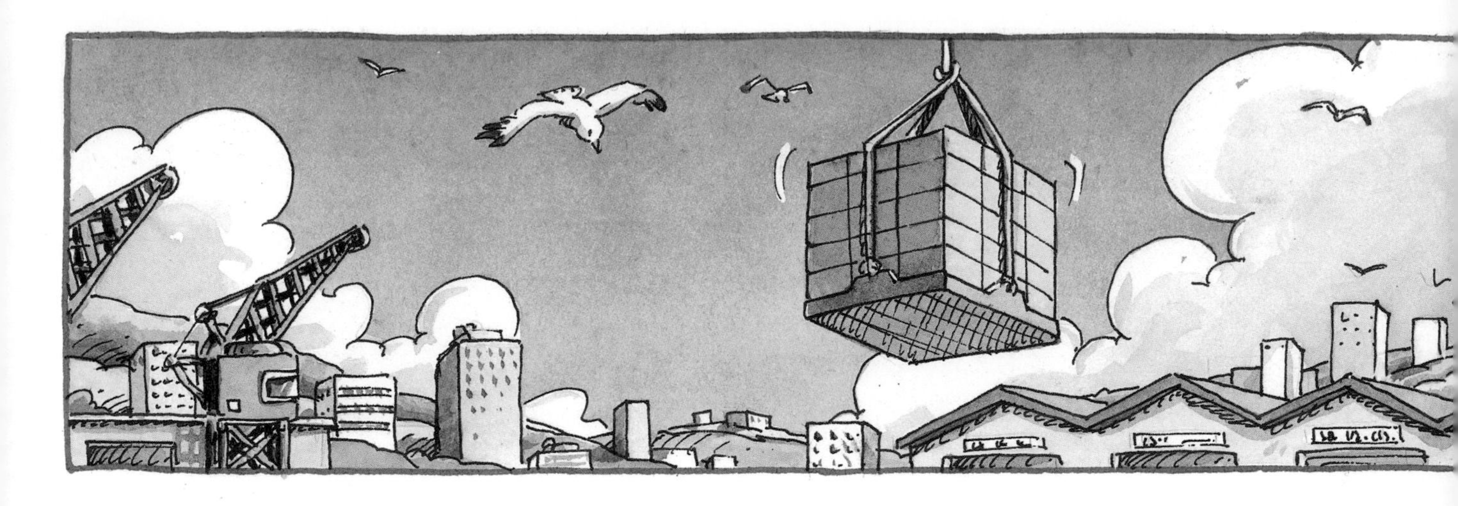

It's very cold and Timmy is ill. Dr Rush came and he looked in Timmy's mouth and listened to his chest with a stethoscope.

He said it's not too bad, and Mummy went to buy some medicine.

I liked the postcard you sent us. There's lots of snow here. Timmy and me made a huge snowman.

Mummy says if I'm good, Father Christmas might bring me a bicycle. That would be great!

Some men from the music shop brought back the old piano today. They have mended it. Mummy is very pleased.

She's going to teach me how to play it. Then when I'm big, I'll be a pianist and go round the world just like you.

When you come home, we'll do all sorts of things together. We can go mushroom-picking in the woods, and fishing in the pond, just like we used to . . .

and at night-time, we'll look up at the sky and you can tell me the story of the little prince who lives on a star.

It’s not long till summer and I know we’ll soon be all together again.

I think about you every day. Please come back quickly.

Love from Sophie

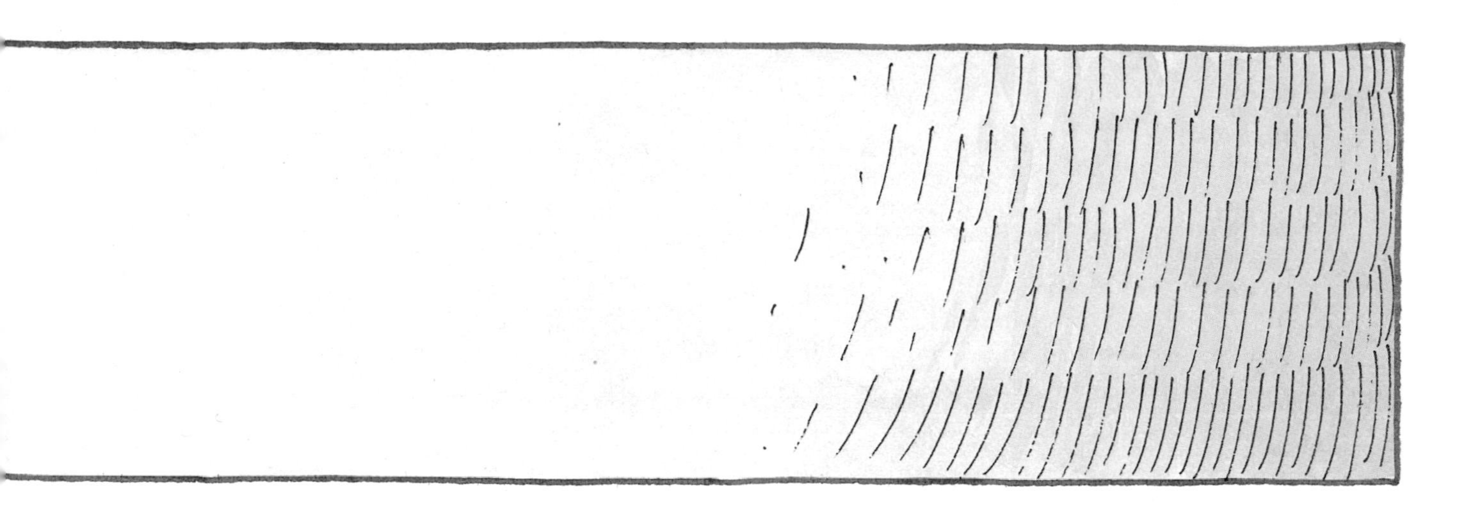

More Andersen Press paperback picture books!